The Tiny Adventures of
Big Sister and Little Sister

illustrations by Crista Kathleen McGinley
story by Marilee Joy Mayfield

Publisher's Cataloging-in-Publication
(Provided by Quality Books, Inc.)

Mayfield, Marilee Joy.
  The tiny adventures of Big Sister and Little Sister / illustrations by Crista Kathleen McGinley ; story by Marilee Joy Mayfield. -- Redwood City, Calif. : Leaping Antelope Productions, 2004.
    p. cm.
    SUMMARY: Big Sister finds everyday life filled with new meaning since Little Sister arrived.
    LCCN 2004102172
    ISBN 0-9659222-2-7

    1. Sisters--Juvenile fiction. [1. Sisters--Fiction.
2. Family--Fiction.]   I. McGinley, Crista Kathleen.
II. Title.

PZ7.M4675Tin 2004   [E]
                  QBI04-200053

To our sisters in life, in heart and in art.

The Tiny Adventures of
Big Sister and Little Sister

My baby sister came home
from the hospital today.

She's asleep now.
I'm trying to be very quiet
even though I'M SO EXCITED.

She is really tiny.

I'm holding my own baby doll,
but now I have a real baby doll instead.

I'm helping Mommy give my little sister a bath today.

The smelly diapers are off
and SUDS ARE EVERYWHERE!

We use a special shampoo
so she won't cry
if it gets in her eyes.

It's amazing how many lotions
and potions we need.

This morning it's BEAUTIFUL outdoors
and we are going for a stroll in the park.

Mommy said I could push the stroller
even though I can barely reach the handle.

We're allowed to take our dog
so he won't feel left out.

Soon my little sister will be GROWN enough
to swing on the swings and

slide down the slide like I do.

Mommy is going to bake cookies today
and we are going to help!

My little sister is crawling already
and she has OPENED UP
ALL of the kitchen cabinets
and TAKEN EVERYTHING OUT.

She likes to put the colander on her head
and **tap out drum sounds**
with a spoon and bowl.

The kitchen smells SO GOOD when we bake.

Today we were in our backyard picking flowers
when something unusual happened.

A green frog jumped out of the grass.

IT SURPRISED US!
First we laughed and then we watched
to see what the frog was doing.
My little sister had *NEVER SEEN* a frog before.

I'll tell Mommy all about the frog
when we go indoors and
give her our bouquet.

Mommy said we could draw, and we have paints in all the colors of the rainbow.

My little sister likes to use her fingers instead of a brush.

I'm painting a flower like the ones in our backyard.

Mommy said our drawings are BEAUTIFUL! When we're finished she's going to put them up on the refrigerator.

My little sister is trying to learn to walk.

She FELL DOWN and scraped her knee.

SHE CRIED SO LOUD.

I put a special bandage on her
and kissed the boo-boo so it will be all better.

Daddy is going to plant in the garden
this afternoon and we get to help.

We have seeds and shovels and pots with baby
plants and NOT-SO-BABY PLANTS
to put in the ground.

My little sister can walk now and I hold her hand.

I really **don't like** bugs,
but my little sister
doesn't seem to mind them.
Ladybugs love her.

We have a chart in our room
and every season we mark it
so we can see how much we've GROWN.

So far, I have more marks than my sister.

I wonder if she will ever be AS TALL AS I AM.

She is trying to stand on her tippy-toes
to look taller.

It's Easter and we get to color LOTS OF eggs.

Mommy prepared our colors for us so we can dip our eggs and make designs and write our names.

I'm giving my best egg design
to my little sister
and I think she's designing
her best egg for me, too.

We're going to make a basket with
marshmallow chickens and bunnies
and chocolates!

I DON'T KNOW WHY, but my little sister likes bugs!

Sometimes we go exploring in our backyard and we capture butterflies and collect caterpillars.

If we catch one, we put it
in a special jar with holes on top
so it can breathe.
After we play, I let the bugs GO FREE.

My little sister wants to keep them all for pets,
but we can't because we catch too many.
Our house would be FILLED WITH BUGS!

We LOVE the summer days
when Daddy takes us to the beach.

My little sister is wearing her
favorite sun bonnet
and I'm wearing my scuba-diving mask.

We're using our plastic pail and shovel
to build a sand castle
near the edge of the ocean.

When we go home we'll have tan and not-so-tan
places when we take off our bathing suits.

Every night before we sleep we say our prayers.

We have a picture of our guardian angel
and she watches over us so we'll be safe.

Even our dog is quiet
while we count our blessings.

We feel cozy and sleepy. ZZZZZZzzzzzz

We have been especially good today.

Mommy said we could put on her perfume, makeup, hats, jewelry and shoes.

It's hard to walk around in these high heels.

We're making LOTS OF NOISE as we CLICK CLACK and CLOMP CLUMP all through the house.

We are having SO MUCH FUN and we look so glamorous!

Today is a special day because it's my birthday.

Our friends are here and we have pizza,
a HUGE CAKE and party favors!

Our dog has joined the party, too.

I CAN'T WAIT TO OPEN ALL MY GIFTS!
My little sister thinks it's her birthday, too,
so I let her help me RIP the **wrapping paper.**

It's raining outdoors.

We've made our own secret tent
and NO ONE KNOWS WHERE WE ARE.

Our lunch tastes better because we're all alone in here.

Even our dog is **NOT ALLOWED** inside our tent.

It's only ENOUGH SPACE for my little sister and me.

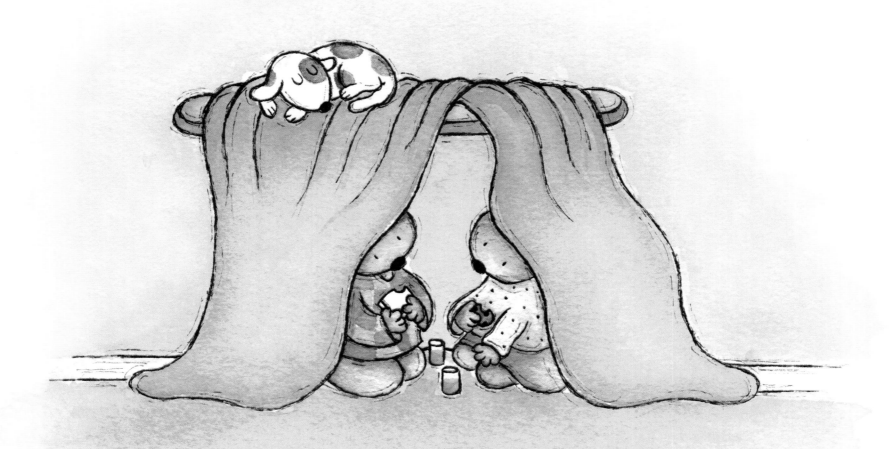

BOOOOoooooo!

It's Halloween!

Time for owls and bats
and BIG BLACK cats.
We're carving faces into PLUMP ORANGE pumpkins
so they can be jack-o'-lanterns.

I'm wearing a witch's hat and a green wig
and I don't think my little sister will know it's me.

If she gets too scared, I'll take off my mask.
We look BOO-tiful in our costumes.

It's too cold and damp
to play outdoors.

But it's a PERFECT day
to listen to our favorite music
and dance, dance, dance!

We KICK OUR HEELS in the air

and we twirl around and around in a circle.

Sometimes we get
a little dizzy.

We feel like we're flying.

It's holiday time and
the snowfl❄kes are falling.

There are BIG PILES of white, fluffy snow and
we are packing it together to make a snowman.

We are soooooooooo cold even though
we're wrapped up in hats, scarves
and our best winter coats.

When we go indoors,
we'll warm up with hot cocoa.

I'm so glad I have a little sister.
I'm so proud to be her BIG SISTER.

We share so many secrets
and we love each other.

I give *my* BEST kisses and hugs to her.

XXXXOOOO

She is the *most special person*
in the world to me!

CRISTA KATHLEEN McGINLEY

is a graduate of the Ringling School of Art and Design. She is an illustrator and the founder of Crista Kathleen Studio, specializing in illustrating children's products and well-loved books. She shares her studio with her kitties, Powder and Tucson.

Crista has always had a vivid imagination filled with child-like magic. As a little girl she could not decide if she wanted to be the tooth fairy or a butterfly. Today Crista lives in Florida with her husband, Vincent. The Big Sister, Little Sister series are her first picture books for Leaping Antelope Productions.

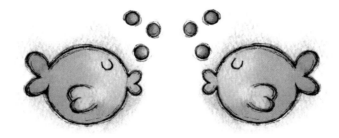

MARILEE JOY MAYFIELD

has been involved in writing, teaching and publishing since she first wrote a series of magazines with her sister, when she was eleven years old and her sister was eight. Marilee's adventures with her two younger sisters are happy memories that were seeds for the Big Sister, Little Sister books.

Today Marilee lives with her husband in Menlo Park, California. They own two businesses together and can kiss each other in the middle of the workday whenever they want.

A Hearts-Beared™ Book